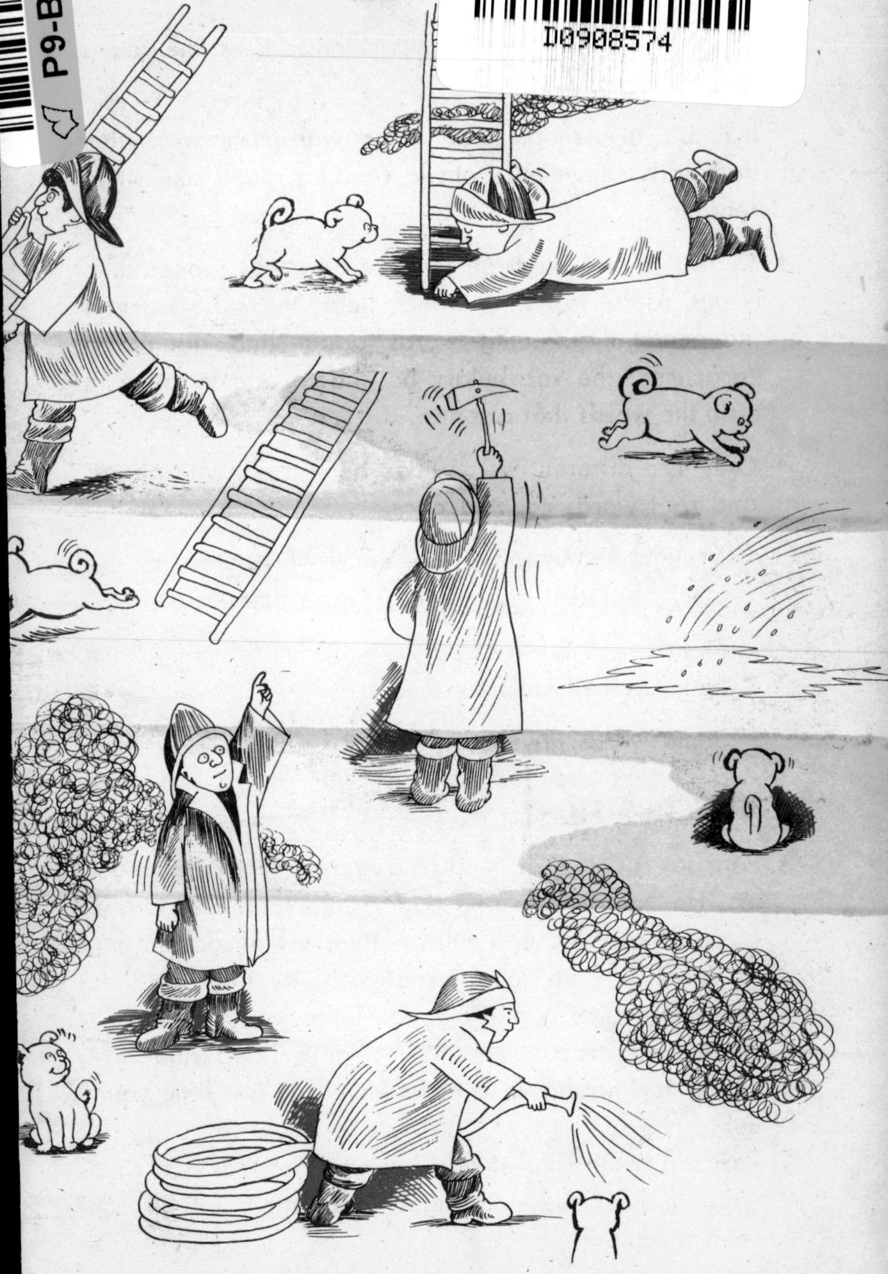

WHY THIS IS AN EASY READER

- This story has been carefully written to keep the young reader's interest high.

- It is told in a simple, open style, with a strong rhythm that adds enjoyment both to reading aloud and silent reading.

- There is a very high percentage of words repeated. It is this skillful repetition which helps the child to read independently. Seeing words again and again, he "practices" the vocabulary he knows, and learns with ease the words that are new.

- Only 178 different words have been used, with plurals and root words counted once.

    Well over one-half of the entire vocabulary of this story has been used at least three times.

    Nearly one-fourth of all the words in this story have been used at least six times.

    Some words have been used 15, 28 and 52 times.

ABOUT THIS STORY

- Popcorn is a natural kind of dog-hero for young readers. He, too, is little and eager, and his world is also big and exciting, and full of situations he doesn't understand. But the young reader is wiser than the little dog, for he knows that Fireman Bill is joking about the spots—and Popcorn doesn't. What a good and rare power feeling that is to have when you are little yourself!

    Popcorn is the kind of dog favorite that makes a child want to hear the story again and again till he can read it himself.

Little Popcorn

Story by SARA ASHERON
Pictures by SUSAN PERL
Editorial Consultant: LILIAN MOORE

WONDER BOOKS

A Division of Grosset & Dunlap, Inc.
New York, N. Y. 10010

Introduction

These books are meant to help the young reader discover what a delightful experience reading can be. The stories are such fun that they urge the child to try his new reading skills. They are so easy to read that they will encourage and strengthen him as a reader.

The adult will notice that the sentences aren't too long, the words aren't too hard, and the skillful repetition is like a helping hand. What the child will feel is: "This is a good story—and I can read it myself!"

For some children, the best way to meet these stories may be to hear them read aloud at first. Others, who are better prepared to read on their own, may need a little help in the beginning—help that is best given freely. Youngsters who have more experience in reading alone—whether in first or second or third grade—will have the immediate joy of reading "all by myself."

These books have been planned to help all young readers grow—in their pleasure in books and in their power to read them.

Lilian Moore
Specialist in Reading
Formerly of Division of Instructional Research,
New York City Board of Education

Library of Congress Catalog Card Number: 68-21297

Text Copyright © 1968, by Sara Asheron.
Illustrations Copyright © 1968, by Grosset & Dunlap, Inc.

Popcorn was a little white dog.

He was white all over —

white as popcorn

popping in a pan.

Popcorn lived on the same street
as the firehouse.

He liked the firehouse

better than anything.

So Popcorn went there every day.

Fireman Bill was his friend.

Every day Fireman Bill said,

"Come in, Popcorn. Come in."

11

Sometimes the firehouse was quiet.

Then Fireman Bill let Popcorn

run around inside.

He let Popcorn

play with the fire hose

around and under . . .

under and around.

Sometimes Fireman Bill let Popcorn
sit up on the fire engine.

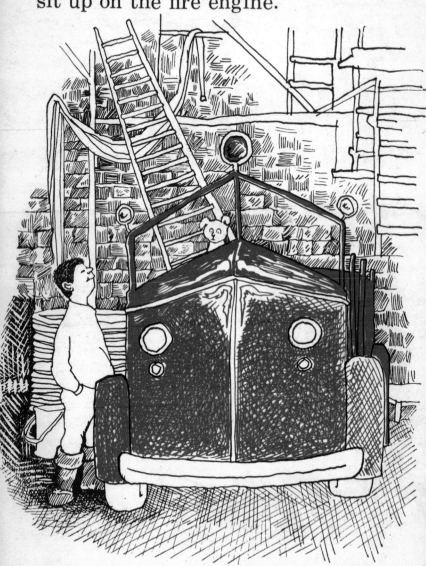

One day he let Popcorn

go up the ladder, too.

But then Fireman Bill had to go up

and bring Popcorn down!

One day Fireman Bill took Popcorn
down the pole—just for the ride.
Popcorn was so happy.

16

"I feel just like a firehouse dog!"
he said to himself.

"I feel like a firehouse dog,"
said Popcorn.
"But I do not LOOK like
a firehouse dog.
I wish I had spots!"
Popcorn looked at himself
in the looking glass.
No spots.
He was white all over—
white as popcorn
popping in a pan.

Sometimes the firehouse was quiet.

But sometimes it was NOT!

Clang!

Clang!

Clang!

Rush!

Rush!

Rush!

Ding-dong!

Then the fire engines went
clanging and rushing out.

Popcorn wanted to run

after the fire engines.

But they were big,

and they went fast.

So Popcorn ran just a little way.

Then he went back to the firehouse
and sat there
till the fire engines came back.

One morning Popcorn

got to the firehouse

just as Fireman Bill got there.

"Woof! Woof!" said Popcorn.

"Good morning to you, too,"

said Fireman Bill.

"You DO like our firehouse, Popcorn,

don't you?"

"Woof! Woof!" said Popcorn.

"Well, come in,"

said Fireman Bill.

"Come in."

Popcorn ran inside.

He jumped up on the fire engine.

He played with the fire hose.

He looked
at the ladder,
but he did NOT
go up.

Fireman Bill had to laugh
at Popcorn.
"You want to be a firehouse dog,
don't you?" he said.

"Woof!" said Popcorn.

"Do you want to ride
with me some day
on the hook-and-ladder truck?"

"Woof! Woof! Woof!" said Popcorn.

Fireman Bill laughed again.
"Well, then," he said,
"try to get some spots, Popcorn.
You get a spot
for every fire you go to,
you know."

27

A spot for every fire!

Popcorn did not know

that Fireman Bill was joking.

The little dog was so happy.

He was going to get some spots.

He was going to look

like a firehouse dog!

Soon after that, there was a fire.

Clang! Clang!

Rush! Rush!

Ding-dong!

The fire engines

went clanging and rushing out.

This time Popcorn was right behind

the fire engines.

He was going to the fire, too.

Today he was going to try

to get a spot!

Clang!

Down the street

went the fire engines.

"Woof!"

Popcorn was right behind.

The firemen ran here and there
with the hose. . .
with the ladders.

Popcorn wanted to help.
He ran around, too—
under the ladders. . .
around and around the hose.

Soon the fire was out.

Popcorn ran all the way home.

He ran right to the looking glass.

He looked at himself.

No spot!

He was white all over—

white as popcorn

popping in a pan.

Popcorn was sad.

"Maybe next time," he said.

Clang! Clang! Clang!

The next time was the next day.

Rush! Rush!

Ding-dong!

Out went the fire engines,

clanging and rushing.

Clang! Clang!

Up the streets

and down the streets.

"Woof! Woof!"

A house was on fire—

a big old house

that no one lived in.

The firemen ran here and there

with the hose. . .

with the ladders.

Popcorn wanted to help.

He ran here and there, too—

under the ladders. . .

around the firemen.

Soon the fire was out.

Popcorn ran all the way home.

He ran to the looking glass.

No spot!

He was white all over—

white as popcorn

popping in a pan.

Popcorn was VERY sad.

"I will try one more time," he said.

"Just one more time."

The next time came soon.

Clang!

Rush!

Ding-dong!

Ding-dong!

Out went the fire engines.

42

"Woof! Woof!"

Out went Popcorn,

right behind them.

This time a little red house
was on fire.
The firemen ran here and there
with the hose. . .

with the ladders.

This time Popcorn did not

run around.

He sat and looked.

Popcorn saw the firemen
go into the house.

He saw them
come out
with a table. . .

with a lamp. . .

with a big looking glass.

He saw the firemen go in.

He saw them come out

with a bird. . .

with a TV set. . .

with a box of books.

"Oh!" said Popcorn.

"So THAT'S the way to help!"

And he ran into the house, too.

"Woof! Woof!" said Popcorn,

"I can't see in here!"

But Popcorn DID see something!
Something the firemen did not see.
Popcorn took it.

Then he ran out of the house.

"Look at the little dog!"

a man called.

Then everyone called out,

"Look! Look at the little dog!"

A girl ran over to Popcorn.

"My doll!" she said.

"Oh, my doll! My doll!"

The girl gave the doll a big hug.

"Thank you, little dog," she said.

She gave Popcorn a big hug, too.

Soon the fire was out.

Popcorn ran over to Fireman Bill.

Fireman Bill looked at Popcorn
and laughed.

"Come here, Popcorn," he said.

"Come and look!"

He took the little dog
over to the looking glass.

Popcorn looked at himself.

What a surprise!

Spots and spots!

Not one. . .

or two. . .

or three. . .

Popcorn had spots ALL over—
just like a firehouse dog!

Popcorn did not

run home THIS time.

This time Popcorn got a ride

all the way back to the firehouse.

Way up on the hook-and-ladder!

Right next to Fireman Bill!

CHOOSE FROM THESE EASY READERS

5901 Will You Come to My Party?

5902 Hurry Up, Slowpoke

5903 Mr. Pine's Mixed-Up Signs

5904 The Adventures of Silly Billy

5905 The Secret Cat

5906 Billy Brown Makes Something Grand

5907 Miss Polly's Animal School

5908 The Duck on the Truck

5909 A Train for Tommy

5910 Surprise in the Tree

5911 The Monkey in the Rocket

5912 Billy Brown: The Baby Sitter

5913 Fly-Away at the Air Show

5914 Arty the Smarty

5915 The Surprising Pets of Billy Brown

5916 Barney Beagle

5917 I Made a Line

5918 Laurie and the Yellow Curtains

5919 Grandpa's Wonderful Glass

5920 Benjamin in the Woods

5921 Barney Beagle Plays Baseball

5922 The Day Joe Went to the Supermarket

5923 Question and Answer Book

5924 Jokes and Riddles

5925 Let Papa Sleep!

5926 The Surprise in the Story Book

5927 The Big Green Thing

5928 The Boy Who Fooled the Giant

5929 More Jokes and Riddles

5930 Too Many Pockets

5931 The Clumsy Cowboy

5932 Cat in the Box

5933 How the Animals Get to the Zoo

5934 The Birthday Party

5935 Little Gray Mouse and the Train

5936 Mr. Pine's Purple House

5937 When I Grow Up

5938 One Kitten is not Too Many

5939 How to Find a Friend

5940 The Boy, the Cat and the Magic Fiddle

5941 Little Gray Mouse Goes Sailing

5942 Keep Your Eyes Open

5945 Old Man and the Tiger

5946 Barbie Goes to a Party

5947 Barney Beagle and the Cat

5948 What's Going on Here?

5949 Little Popcorn

5951 The Fox Who Traveled

5952 The Three Coats of Benny Bunny